AMERICAN TALL TALES

Casey Jones

Retold by M. J. York ❧ Illustrated by Michael Garland

The Child's World®
1980 Lookout Drive • Mankato, MN 56003-1705
800-599-READ • www.childsworld.com

Acknowledgments
The Child's World®: Mary Berendes, Publishing Director
The Design Lab: Kathleen Petelinsek, Design
Red Line Editorial: Editorial direction

ISBN 9781614732099
LCCN 2012932261

Printed in the United States of America
Mankato, MN
July 2012
PA02124

Way back in the olden days, before folks had cars and airplanes to get around, the fastest way to get from place to place was by train. Every train had an engineer—the driver who decided when to slow down or speed up. And the fastest engineer in the country, maybe the fastest engineer ever, was Casey Jones.

Casey was born loving trains. Why, you never found young Casey without a toy train in his hand and a little engineer's cap on his head. He spent all his free time hanging around the train yard. At the tender age of fifteen, he got himself his first job with the railroad sending telegraphs. But he still dreamed of one day driving his own train.

Casey became a brakeman—that's the worker who sets the brakes and waves the signal flag.

Then he became a fireman. On a train, the fireman doesn't put out fires. On a train, the fireman makes the fire, shoveling coal into the furnace to keep the steam engine running.

At last, Casey was an engineer, driving a train of his own. But he wasn't quite happy yet. You see, he was driving a slow freight train. And freight trains always had to get out of the way for more important trains. What Casey really

wanted was to run a passenger train, the fastest passenger train in the country.

After years of hard work, Casey finally reached his dream. He was an engineer for the Illinois Central Line, and he ran the fastest passenger train in the country. He loved pushing in the throttle and going as fast as he could, watching the farms and fields and towns go blurry outside the window.

Folks always knew when Casey was coming. He had a certain way of blowing his whistle, starting loud and wild like a howling wolf and trailing off sweet and slow like a lullaby. Fussy babies went to sleep with a smile on their faces when they heard Casey's whistle.

But even if they didn't hear Casey's whistle, folks still knew when he was coming because Casey was always on time. They set their clocks by Casey's schedule. Rain or even a late start couldn't stop Casey, no sir. With the throttle down and his nimble brakeman, Sim Weber, at the furnace, Casey could beat any engineer's time on any route. Folks say Casey's train flew by so fast, you could put an egg in a frying pan next to the

track and find it cooked sunny-
side up after Casey went by.

Once, Casey and Sim
were driving the mail car to
Memphis, Tennessee, and they
almost didn't make it on time.
It was raining like the sky was
falling, and the tracks were
nearly flooded.

Sim said, "Casey, we've got to
slow down!"

"No, Sim," replied Casey. "We
can make it!" His hand stayed
on the throttle, and the train

stayed on the tracks. They sprinted into Memphis just as the clock chimed seven—on time on the dot. At the station, the other engineers were amazed.

"That Casey," they said. "Don't you ever doubt he'll be on time. Through night and rain and snow and fog, he'll always make it."

Now, Casey and Sim were plum tired after that run, and they wanted nothing more than a hot cup of tea and a warm bed for the night. But the station master came up to Casey, and he needed a favor. The engineer for the southbound passenger train to Canton, Mississippi, had fallen sick and couldn't make his run. Casey was dead tired, but the station master didn't have to ask him twice. And loyal Sim wasn't about to let Casey go without him.

They rushed down to the train and pulled out of the station. Trouble was, starting out they were already running an hour and half late.

"We'll never make up that much time," said Sim to Casey.

But Casey just shook his head and smiled. "We'll just have to go a little faster," he replied.

So they went. Casey leaned down on the throttle with all his might, easing up only the tiniest bit for the worst curves. You could feel the train lean hard away from the turn, but the wheels held on the track, and the train kept speeding through the night. Sim shoveled coal like a madman, working harder than he'd ever worked in his life to keep the engine fired up.

And as they blazed through stations on the way, it looked as if it were working. They made up five minutes, then fifteen, then fifty. They made up an hour and fifteen minutes— only fifteen minutes late. They tore up the tracks, with Casey highballing all the way, pushing the train as fast as it would go.

But now comes the sad part of our tale. Casey was steaming along faster than fast when he came screeching around a curve and saw a light on the tracks where no light should be. It was another train, and there was no way Casey could stop in time.

"Jump, Sim," he yelled, hauling hard on the brake. And Sim jumped, landing away from the tracks safely. But did Casey jump? No, sir. Noble Casey knew the passengers in his train

would die if he saved himself. So he just pulled harder on the brake, hoping and praying he'd stop in time.

But Casey's best was not enough. The trains collided with a CRASH heard all the way in Memphis. And Casey died with the brake tight in his hand. But Casey slowed that train enough that it stayed on the track. And even though Casey died up in the engine, all the passengers back in the cars were safe.

Some say if you walk by the tracks on the old Illinois Central Line on a soft summer's evening, sometimes you'll feel a rush of air and hear a faint whistle. That's just Casey, trying to get his passengers to Canton on time.

BEYOND THE STORY

Casey Jones is an American tall tale. Tall tales are exaggerated stories, and can be based on actual events and people or can be fictional but close to real life. Exaggerations (or telling things a bit larger, better, scarier, and so on than they really were) are key elements in tall tales. In fact, that's how they get their names. The stories are "tall" because they are larger than normal life.

Casey Jones is a tall tale based on a true story. The character Casey Jones lived from 1863 to 1900; his full name was John Luther Jones, but everyone called him Casey because he lived near Cayce, Kentucky. He was a fast-driving railroad engineer, just like in the story. But there are a few things the tale's narrator exaggerates: such as when Casey blows his whistle and babies go "chugga-chugga, whoo-whoo," and when he passes by houses and foods get cooked because he's going so fast.

Alas, the story of his train crash and death is true. Casey Jones died on April 30, 1900, when his train, named "Cannonball Express" collided with another train in Vaughan, Mississippi, on a rainy night. But Casey's heroism is true, too. He alone stayed aboard the train to hold onto the break lever to save everyone in the other train. And from this heroic act, he became a legend, and a story that turned into the tall tale you are hearing today.

If you want to learn more about the real man behind this tall tale, there are two museums dedicated to his honor in Mississippi: the Historic Casey Jones Home & Railroad Museum, and the Water Valley Casey Jones Railroad Museum.

ABOUT THE AUTHOR

M. J. York has an undergraduate degree in English and history and a master's degree in library science. M. J. lives in Minnesota and works as a children's book editor. She has always been fascinated by myths, legends, and fairy tales from around the world.

ABOUT THE ILLUSTRATOR

Michael Garland is a best-selling author and illustrator with thirty books to his credit. He has received numerous awards and his recent book, *Miss Smith and the Haunted Library*, made the New York Times Best Sellers list. Michael has illustrated for celebrity authors such as James Patterson and Gloria Estefan, and his book *Christmas Magic* has become a season classic. Michael lives in New York with his family.